Very little Rapunzel

Teresa Heapy & Sue Heap

For Mum and Dad - T. H.

For Pen and Greg - S. H.

PICTURE CORGI

UK | USA | Canada | Ireland | Australia
India | New Zealand | South Africa
Picture Corgi is part of the Penguin Random House group of companies
whose addresses can be found at global.penguinrandomhouse.com.
www.penguin.co.uk   www.puffin.co.uk   www.ladybird.co.uk

Penguin
Random House
UK

First published 2017
001

Printed in China
A CIP catalogue record for this book is available from the British Library

ISBN: 978-1-782-95314-2

All correspondence to:
Picture Corgi, Penguin Random House Children's
80 Strand, London WC2R 0RL

Very Little Rapunzel
lived in a tall tower.

She needed a haircut.

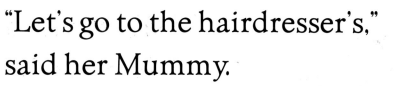

"Let's go to the hairdresser's,"
said her Mummy.

"No, I **not** haircut,"
said Very Little Rapunzel.

Big Box
of
Hair
Things

Things

"Well, let's try a different *style*," said her Mummy.

So they tried ...

a dried style,

a tied style,

a reaching-
to-the-sky style,

a plait style,

a flat style,

a put-on-a-big-hat style,

a bun
style,

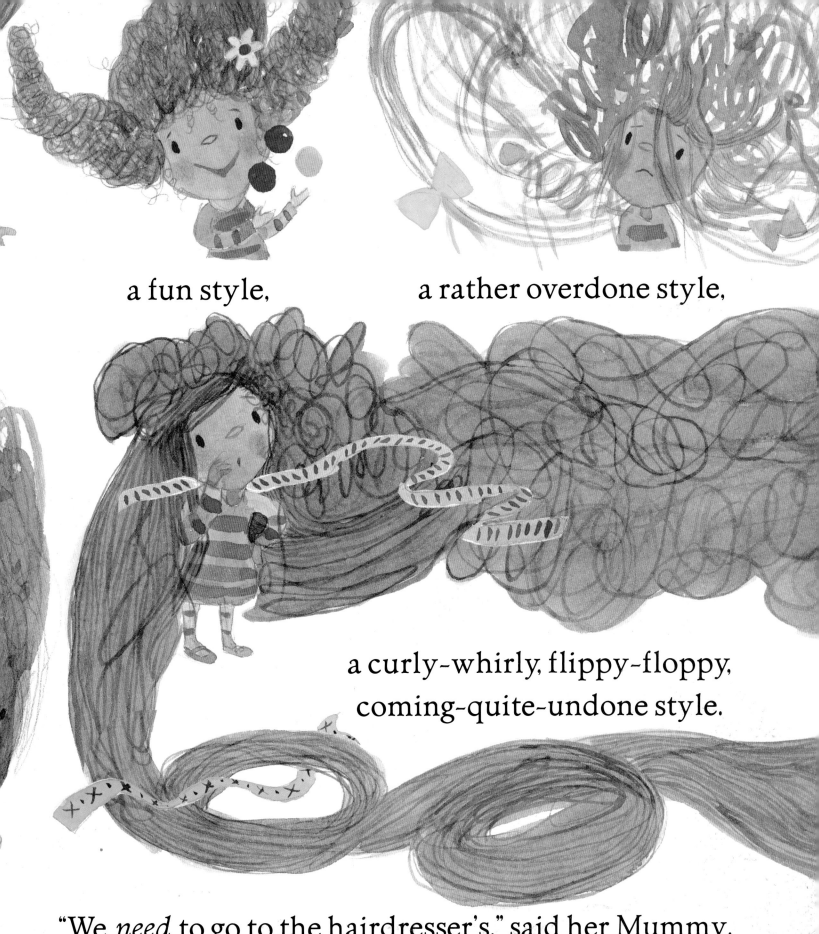

a fun style, a rather overdone style,

a curly-whirly, flippy-floppy,
coming-quite-undone style.

"We *need* to go to the hairdresser's," said her Mummy.

"No!" said Very Little Rapunzel.

And she threw the
Big Box of Hair Things
right out of the window.

It was a very

l
  o
    o
      o
        o
          o
            n
              g
                way
                  down.

"I'm sorry, Mummy,"
said **Very** Little Rapunzel.

She pulled her hair into the tower.

Now, at the bottom
of the tower, there was
a **Very** <small>Little</small> **Prince**.

Big Box
of
Hair
things

and the **Very** Little Prince climbed all the way up.

Very Little Rapunzel
and the Very Little Prince
tried to have a Play.

It was a bit hard.

And then
Very Little Rapunzel
scratched her head.

"Mummy," she said, "my head all *itchy*."
"And me!" said the Very Little Prince.

Very Little Rapunzel's
Mummy had a quick look.

OH NO!

she said.

"I'm afraid, my loves, you've got . . .

"NITS!"

Very Little Rapunzel's Mummy started scratching her own head.

"**You** got nits too?"
said Very Little Rapunzel.

"I think we need the Special Comb,"
said her Mummy.

"That **too** tiny!"
said Very Little Rapunzel.

"This is going to take a VERY
long time . . ." said her Mummy.

Very Little Rapunzel's Mummy
combed and combed and combed
Very Little Rapunzel's **very** long hair.

YEOOW

yelled Very Little Rapunzel.

After the combing, it was hair-wash time.

"I do this!"

said Very Little Rapunzel.

"I put all my hair on the top,
and I get the big jug
and I tip it **right up** and ..."

SPLASH!

"I think we need a bigger towel," said her Mummy.

"Maybe my hair is too much in the way," said Very Little Rapunzel to the Very Little Prince.

One minute later,
her Mummy turned back—
and Very Little Rapunzel's long hair was
all gone.

"Oh my goodness ...
look at your **hair!**"
gasped her Mummy.

No more
hair —
no more
nits!

"But," said the **Very** Little **Prince**,
"no hair means NO climbing!
How do I get DOWN?"

The **Very** <small>Little</small> Prince started to cry.
"I come give you a hug!" said
Very <small>Little</small> Rapunzel.
She ran over to him and . . .

WHOOPS!

she slipped on the slippy-wet floor.

"Now **that** makes me an idea…"
said Very Little Rapunzel,
"to get down from our tower!"

And so the Very Little Prince,
Very Little Rapunzel
and her Mummy got the
Big Box of Hair Things.

Big Box
of
Hair
Things

Big Box of Hair Things

Extra- -Super- -Duper-

And with plaiting and pinning,
and a lot of **Extra-Super-Duper-Strong Hair Spray** …

... they made a super-slippy hairslide for the tower.

Very Little Rapunzel and the Very Little Prince went down and came up again, and again, and again.

They whizzed and they slipped,
they whooshed and they flipped,